1041

BY DAVID GULASI

CONTENT WARNING

This book contains extreme graphic violence, mature sexual themes, disturbing psychological horror, and unrelenting dread.

Reader discretion is strongly advised.

"And if you gaze long into an abyss,
the abyss also gazes into you."

— Friedrich Nietzsche

Tiptoe through the tulips with me...

Tiptoe through the tulips with me...

Tiptoe through the tulips with m...

Tiptoe through the tulips wit...

Tiptoe through the tuli...

Tiptoe through th...

Tiptoe throu...

Tipte thr...

Tip...

TABLE OF CONTENTS

CONTENT WARNING..3

CHAPTER 1 Good Morning......................................1

CHAPTER 2 The Farm..12

CHAPTER 3 Kate..26

CHAPTER 4 Suki..40

CHAPTER 5 Bonjo..51

CHAPTER 6 The Dinner...64

CHAPTER 7 Destination..79

CHAPTER 8 Good Night...86

CHAPTER 9 The Surgeon.....................................105

AUTHOR'S NOTE...116

CHAPTER 1
Good Morning

So this is how it ends. Me lying down on a motel room bed, with my dick out, choking to death. Oh what lows I have reached in my life to get to this fucking point.

Gasping for air, hands on my throat, trying to see what's happening. Nothing is grabbing me but it feels like—my body is on fire. Burning from the inside out. My face—something's ripping it apart. Tearing at the skin. Pulling it off in strips. The pain is unbearable.

Can still hear the Japanese porn running on the screen. Yamete (Stop), yamete (stop). How fucked is it to die with that sound in the background? Not birds. Not my loved ones. No. Just a small Asian woman being annihilated by a giant Black man.

Need air, not porn. Stand up, try to look in the mirror. See my throat being pressed down by hands. What fucking hands? Need air.

Fall to the ground. The air is gone. My lungs burn.

Vision goes black at the edges. Spreading inward like ink in water.

The last thing I see is my own pathetic face in the mirror—red, bulging, dying.

The last thing I hear is yamete, yamete.

Nothing.

Everything goes black.

Wake up gasping.

My throat just... opens. Like someone flipped a switch. Air floods in and it burns going down but I don't care because I'm breathing again.

I'm on the bathroom floor. Tile cold against my cheek. Spit and drool pooled under my face.

That smell. God awful smell. I look and yes—I shit myself. Fuck me! It's mixed with the smell of a dog. Smells like a big drooling musky dog mixed with my shit.

Need to clean up. Can't go out like this.

I pull myself up. Turn on the shower. Step in before the water even warms.

It hits my skin.

Good Morning

FUCK!

Not hot. Boiling. Like stepping into a pot of water that's been on the stove too long.

I grit my teeth. Stay under it. Scrub fast. The water scalding every inch of me. My skin turning red. Blistering.

But I need this shit off me.

Thirty seconds. That's all I can take. I jump out. My skin screaming.

Grab a towel. Pat down carefully. Everything hurts.

I stumble to the sink. My legs are shaking so bad I almost go down again. Grip the edge to steady myself. My reflection looks like shit—face all red, eyes bloodshot, hair stuck to my forehead. Skin pink and raw from the water.

Then I see my neck.

Red marks. Finger-shaped. Five on one side, thumb on the other. Like someone actually grabbed me and squeezed.

I touch them, massaging the skin, still trying to catch my breath.

But as I'm staring at them, they start to fade.

It's weird as hell—the redness just drains away. First the edges blur, then the whole thing softens, gets lighter, and then it's just... gone. Ten seconds and my neck looks completely normal. Like nothing ever happened.

What the fuck?

I sit down hard on the toilet lid. Still naked. Still trying to process.

Coughing, spitting, trying to figure out what the hell just happened.

What the fuck was that?

That's when I hear it from the bedroom.

A groan. Deep. That satisfied male porn star grunt.

The porn finished.

I turn and look through the doorway. The screen still glowing. The guy pulls out and sprays all over her face. Like rain. Like he's watering a fucking plant.

No clue what's going on. Like seriously, one minute I'm beating my meat watching porn, next thing I'm suffocating. That's around the time the lights were flickering. Like what the fuck?

I just almost died. I saw hands choking me that weren't even there. I watched my own throat getting crushed in the mirror.

And now I'm sitting here naked on a motel toilet watching the money shot of porn I don't even remember putting on.

I look at the time. 10:41:01 on my Casio watch.

That's strange.

Oh fuck. The meeting. I need to get to the meeting. I'm late.

I quickly dress. My throat still hurts—sharp, like I swallowed glass. What the hell just happened?

The room looks worse in daylight. Old. Green carpet worn down to the padding in spots. Dark purple and green wallpaper peeling at the corners, probably original to the building. 1970s motel decay. The shower's dripping. Drip. Drip. Drip. Constant. Maddening. The window's half open, yellowed curtain barely moving.

Wait. This isn't a hotel. It's a motel.

I remember now. I drove here last night. Late. Needed somewhere to crash before the morning meeting.

I think.

I grab my suit jacket off the chair. It looks like it was on special at Walmart for ten bucks. Wrinkled. Smells like cigarette smoke even though I don't smoke.

I bump into the bed. Something rattles—metal on metal—and falls to the floor with a clang.

The coin box.

The thing you're supposed to feed quarters into to make the bed vibrate. "Magic Fingers" or whatever the fuck they called it.

I grab my room key off the nightstand.

Room 1041.

I stare at it.

1041

My watch: 10:41.

The room: 1041.

That's... that's a weird coincidence.

I shake my head. No time for this. The meeting.

Outside, the air hits me like a wall. Hot. Humid. Smells like rotting fruit and exhaust.

The cleaning lady is there. She's in her fifties, maybe older—hard to tell. Looks like she's had ten kids and not enough energy to look after any of them. But she moves fast. Automatic. Like she's said the same words a thousand times.

"Hey," I say. "Good morning." I'm trying to remember her name. For some strange reason I feel like I should know it. She looks familiar.

"Good morning, Mr. Gutani. How was your sleep?"

She knows me. Of course she does.

I look at her. My neck still sore. I rub it and say, "Good, thanks."

We both know it's a lie. She can probably see it on my face. It's just one of those things you say, I guess.

She moves past me with her cart, muttering something under her breath. Sounds like Spanish. Or maybe Portuguese? I can't tell.

I pat my jacket pocket.

Empty.

"Oh, Mariana—have you seen my keys?"

She stops. Reaches into her apron pocket and pulls out a set of keys. Old. Tarnished metal. A Cadillac logo on the fob.

"You mean these, sir?"

"Yes. Thank you."

I take them from her. Our fingers brush for a second.

She stares at me. Really stares. Then her hand goes to the cross hanging around her neck. She grips it tight, brings it to her lips, and mutters something. Spanish, I think? Or was it Colombian? Wait, do Colombians speak Spanish? I'm an idiot and I'm late.

"You okay?" I ask.

She doesn't answer. Just pushes her cart away faster than before.

What the fuck was that about?

I look around the parking lot.

Where's my car?

Black. I remember it being black. But what model? What year?

Why can't I remember my own car?

There. I see it.

Parked under an apple tree. Bright red apples hanging low, almost touching the roof.

The car is a black 1960 Cadillac with a red racing stripe down the center. Chrome gleaming even in the shade.

I don't remember owning this.

But the key fits.

I walk toward it. The apples look perfect. Too perfect. Glossy and red like they're waxed. None of them have fallen. Not one rotting apple on the ground beneath the tree. Just perfect red fruit hanging there, untouched.

"I wouldn't, Mr. Gutani."

I turn. Mariana is watching me from across the lot.

"There's a snake in that tree."

I look up. For a second I see something move. A ripple through the branches. Dark. Quick. Then nothing. Just apples.

"Thanks."

She clutches her cross again. Mutters something I can't hear.

The car door creaks open like it hasn't been used in years. I slide in. The leather seats are cracked, stuffing poking through in places. Smells like old cigars and something sweet. Rotten sweet. The dashboard is dusty but the steering wheel is clean. Like someone's been driving it recently. But the seats feel like they haven't been sat in for years.

There's a black suitcase on the passenger seat. I don't remember putting it there. I reach over, try the locks. Four-digit code. I spin the numbers. Nothing. What's the code? I can't remember.

I throw my jacket on top of it and slide the key into the ignition. The engine starts. Quiet. Too quiet for a car this old.

The radio crackles to life.

Static first. Then a voice.

High-pitched. Warbling. Unnatural.

"Tiptoe through the tulips, with meeee..."

I freeze.

The song continues. That fucking ukulele. That voice that sounds like it's coming from a broken music box.

"Tiptoe through the tulips, with meeee..."

My hand shoots out. I twist the radio knob.

Off.

Silence.

My heart is pounding.

Why the fuck would that song be playing?

I shake my head. Just a weird oldies station. That's all.

I put the car in reverse and back out of the motel driveway, drive pass the other rooms and also the cleaning lady who is still staring at me

As I pull away, I glance in the rearview mirror.

The cleaning lady is standing in the middle of the parking lot. Not moving. Just watching me, Her hand is still on her cross, her lips moving, muttering something like a maniac.

Even from here, through the dust and distance, I can see her lips moving. Still praying. Still watching me drive away, I'm out of here I need to get to my meeting.

CHAPTER 2
The Farm

Driving around the corner from the motel, in a hurry, my wheels scratch against the curb. Metal scraping concrete. No time to check for damage. I'm late. Late for my meeting.

Wait. What time did it start?

The suitcase is still on the passenger seat. Maybe the meeting time is written in there somewhere.

Using one hand while I drive, I try to unlock the bag. It won't budge. Locked with a four-digit code.

Fuck. What's the code? I can't remember.

Anyway, I'll get to that later. The ride is long. I'm so thirsty. So damn thirsty. I need some water. Any water. This is one long lane stretching ahead into nothing. No left turns. No right turns. No buildings on either side of the road.

Just fog. I can't even see beyond it. It's daytime and there's fog. No—not fog. Steam. The road is clear but covered in this shit.

Thick. Strange. Not the cool morning kind—this fog is hot. Muggy. It sits heavy on everything like wet cloth.

The AC doesn't work. Windows cracked open just enough to let in air that's somehow worse than what's trapped inside. Humid. Sticky. Smells like smoke and rot.

How did I get out this far?

It feels like a strange day.

Through the fog, I can see a red glow in the distance. Bleeding through the haze. Sky stained orange and sick. For some reason I know I have to get there. That's where I'm meant to be. YES. I remember now. Do I remember? That's where my meeting is held. Feels good knowing I didn't forget everything.

Apparently, I'm driving straight toward it.

Sweat drips down my back. The steering wheel is slick under my palms.

As I reach the lower end of the long strip, finally something. A small house. No—not a house. A farm. White house with a paddock in the back and a shed. Weathered wood. Peeling paint. McLaren's Farm, the sign reads.

BANG.

I look for the origin of the sound. Was it a tire? The hood?

BANG.

There it goes again. The car's done. That ain't normal.

I slow down. As the car comes to a stop, smoke pours out of the exhaust, mixing with the fog.

I crack the door open and step out into the heat. The fog mixed with the heat is torture. I wipe my forehead with my sleeve and walk towards the old house. Looking around—there's no one here. Not a sound. Not a person. Not even insects. I walk up the creaky porch.

"HELLO!" I shout toward the farmhouse, really hoping someone would hear me.

It looks quiet. Too damn quiet. I don't think they heard me. I scream again. "HELLO! ANYONE THERE?!"

Why am I screaming? I should just go up and knock on the door.

Which I do.

I knock. Then another knock. Then I bang on the door. I try to look inside but the house looks deserted. Like no one's been here in ages.

I try opening the door. It's locked.

I think I'll have to go around the back.

I turn.

He's just standing there.

I don't know how long he's been there. Behind me. Close. Too close. I didn't hear him come up. Like a damn ninja.

A man. Tall. Thin in a way that looks wrong—like something stretched him out. Overalls hanging loose on a frame that's all bone and sinew. Straw hat casting a shadow over most of his face. Piece of wheat hanging from his mouth, moving slightly as he breathes.

His hands are huge. Coarse. Calloused. Stained dark—dirt or blood, I can't tell. The damn smell of sweat, shit, piss and rot coming off him like a fan in summer.

He doesn't blink. Just stares. Breathing steadily.

"You ain't s'posed to be here," he says. Voice low. Slow. Like he's chewing each word before letting it out.

My heart is hammering. "I know, I'm sorry. My car broke down. I'm on my way to a meeting." I point toward the red glow.

He slowly—so slowly—turns his head. Looks at the glow. Then back at me. His eyes are pale. Watery. Empty.

He looks me up and down. Takes his time. Like he's deciding something.

"You should be headin' out now."

"I will, but can I use your phone? Please. I just want to make a call and then I'll be heading out."

He doesn't answer right away. Just keeps staring. The wheat in his mouth moves up and down.

"Phone's 'round back," he finally says. "Come on."

He walks back down the porch. Doesn't look to see if I'm following. Just assumes I will.

I follow.

That's when I see them.

Two large black Dobermans. Mating.

And the strange part? They're both looking at me. Not at each other. At me. This is fucking weird.

I smile and say, "Nice dogs." I had two sets of eyes on me. One slightly smaller and a much larger dog hammering away, like I wasn't even there.

The farmer keeps walking. Doesn't respond.

We reach the back shed. He enters and sits on a wooden chair.

"There's the phone." He points toward the back of the metallic shed.

"You mean in that place?" I asked.

He didn't respond. Just proceeded to point and then continue chewing whatever the fuck he was chewing. I came closer to the shed. Damn.

It smells like—

Oh. Dead pigs. All over the place. Hanging from hooks. Must be where they're chopped.

"Thank you, sir," I say nervously, but still wondering why the phone is here and not inside.

He sits there. Spits. Wipes his nose. "Go on, git to it."

I look down at the phone and realize I don't know what number to call.

I look at my watch. 10:41:02. That's got to be wrong. I tap it. Definitely broken.

The phone is an old rotary. The kind where you have to rotate the numbers.

I'm thinking, what's the number?

As I'm doing that, I look up.

The man is gone.

Then I hear it.

A loud squeal. High-pitched. Desperate.

Followed by the sound of cracking bones.

The squeal gets louder. Closer.

The farmer comes back through the door. I'm still holding the phone handle in one hand.

He's dragging a pig.

Its legs are all broken. Front and back. Bone jutting out through skin. White shards poking through bloody flesh.

"Wait," I say. "What are you doing? Can you wait for me to leave? Please?"

He looks up at me. Then grabs the pig by its front leg —the broken one—and lifts.

The bone shifts. The cartilage stretches. The pig screams.

Blood drips onto the concrete floor. Thick. Dark red, almost black.

I put the phone down. "I need to leave."

The door is closed.

He stares at me. Spits on the ground.

"We need to do this so you can make that call. This shit ain't free."

He continues to lift the pig—completely onto the bench. Only three feet from where I'm standing.

The pig is thrashing. Screaming. Its broken legs flailing, bone scraping against metal.

Then, with a knife—long, rusted at the hilt—he slits the pig's throat.

Deep. Ear to ear.

The sound is a loud squeal, then a wet gurgling. Like it's choking on its own blood.

Blood sprays. Hits the wall. Hits the floor. Some of it hits my shoes.

The pig's eyes are wide. Rolling back. Its body convulsing.

The blood pours out. Thick. Steaming in the heat. Pooling on the bench, dripping onto the floor in heavy streams.

The gurgling continues. Wet. Choking. The pig's mouth opening and closing, trying to breathe through the flood.

"I don't need to make a call anymore. Sorry. I'll be leaving now."

He blocks the path.

"You need to make that call," he says. Grinning. Rotten teeth. "Otherwise you ain't goin' nowhere, son."

He starts laughing.

I go back. The phone lights up. A light that wasn't there before is there now. I pick up the handle.

I dial the first numbers that come to mind. I don't even know what number to call.

- 1 Turn. Click back.

- 0 Turn. Click back.

- 4 Turn. Click back.

- 1 Turn. Click back.

It's the first thing that came to mind.

It rings.

Then the crackling voice. A voice in the distance. I can barely hear it. I heard "get him ready," then the crackling sound and then—

"Hello?" A voice on the other side. It was a deep male voice.

"Hello," I say. "Hi, I'm Jaso—"

The voice doesn't let me finish.

"Ah yes, Mr. Gutani. Your reservation has been set. Please make your way back on the road and head our way. Your car should be ready."

"Our way?" I ask. "Where is 'our'—"

The phone hangs up.

I look up.

The farmer opens the door. The pig carcass is still on the bench. Dead now. Blood still dripping. The body of the pig shrivelled like its entire organs have been removed. Almost burnt out.

I notice the rats climbing up the bench legs, already eating the entrails spilling out from where he gutted it, their squeaking mixing with the steady drip of blood hitting the concrete.

I try to move toward the door, slow and careful, like if I move too fast something bad will happen.

The farmer's eyes lock onto mine and he doesn't say anything at first, just stares at me with those pale, watery eyes that look right through me. Then his mouth stretches into something that might be a smile, showing those rotten teeth.

He just stared at me. No emotions. Just a grin like he was happy about something.

Then he starts laughing—low and wet, like something's rattling around in his chest.

I can smell his breath from here and it's awful, like rot and decay, like something died in his mouth and never left.

I creep past him and he doesn't move, just watches me the whole way with those empty eyes following every step I take.

I get out of the shed and the dogs are waiting for me.

Both of them sitting there, perfectly still, staring at me like they've been told to wait for something.

Not barking, not moving, just watching with this intense focus that makes my skin crawl.

I walk past them carefully, every step deliberate, trying not to show how terrified I am.

I look at them and put out my hand. Like an idiot I say, "Good doggies." My voice cracks. "You ain't gonna hurt me, are ya?"

Their growls start low and deep in their chests, this rumble I can feel in my bones, and I know I'm fucked.

"Right. You stupid fucks."

I run for it and the barking explodes behind me—loud, vicious, getting closer with every second.

I can hear their claws scraping against the dirt and they're fast, so much faster than I thought they'd be, and I'm running as hard as I can but they're gaining on me.

I reach the car and yank the door open, jump in, try to slam it shut—

But it won't close because the dog has its head stuck inside, jaws snapping, teeth gnashing inches from my leg, spit flying everywhere, eyes wild and crazy, foam dripping from its mouth.

It's barking so loud I can't think straight, the sound filling the entire car, and I can feel its hot breath on my skin.

I lean back and kick it hard in the teeth, as hard as I can.

It yelps and pulls back, taking part of my shoe with it —the leather ripped clean off.

I slam the door shut and lock it, my hands shaking so bad I can barely get the key in the ignition.

I need to breathe, just breathe, but my lungs are burning and my throat still hurts from this morning and my heart is hammering so hard against my ribs I think it might actually burst. I'm so thirsty. I need water. My lips are as dry as a desert. I need something. I don't even have spit in my mouth.

"Get it together, man. Get it together, Jason."

I start the car and it worked. I was happy. But I thought —what did he mean by the reservation is ready?

I hit the accelerator, the car lurching forward, gravel spraying everywhere.

I don't look back at first, I just drive, hands white-knuckled on the steering wheel, sweat dripping down my face.

Then I do look back, in the rearview mirror.

The farmer is standing in the middle of the road, not moving, just standing there like a scarecrow.

The two dogs sit on either side of him, perfectly still, like statues, like they're not even real animals anymore.

All three of them watch me drive away and they don't move, don't chase, just stand there in the fog.

As I get farther away they get smaller and smaller, fading into that thick, hot fog.

Until they're gone completely, swallowed up by the haze, like they were never there at all.

CHAPTER 3
Kate

Hit that accelerator. Late. Fucking late. The suitcase was still there. Went to open it again—locked. Still didn't remember the password. Kept going down the highway, engine roaring. Wasn't going to stop until I got there.

Just like that, a speck appeared in the distance. Not stopping, I said to myself.

That's when I saw her. Golden hair reflecting the light. She was absolutely beautiful.

Something about the way she smiled at nothing. Open. Trusting. Like she'd never seen real danger. Like she wouldn't see it coming.

Having a messed up day, everything turning to shit, she was probably crazy as well. But standing out here in this heat, in this fog that wouldn't lift, on a road I didn't remember taking—maybe crazy was exactly what I needed right now.

Drove past her. Did, however, turn my head just as I was passing, and everything slowed down. Her blue eyes. Her flowing hair in the wind. Her glowing skin and tall, slim build. Her expression went from bright to dim the moment I passed her.

Hit the brakes. Automatically. Without even thinking, my body reacted before I could even put a thought in.

The dust mixed with the hot fog went all around the car. As the dust surrounded everything, she appeared out of it. There she was, fixing her hair, smiling, asking to get into my car with her eyes.

Leaned over and unlocked the door. She opened it and slid in, the hot air from outside rushing in with her, but somehow she brought cool with her, like she'd been standing in shade I couldn't see. Before she spoke, the first thing was her smell—coconuts, sweet and clean, nothing like the rot and smoke that had been choking me all day.

"You're an angel," her first words.

"I was burning out there."

"You're welcome. I'm heading over to my meeting." Signalled ahead toward the bright red glow.

"Yeah, I'm also heading that way," she replied.

"Oh great," I said enthusiastically, knowing I didn't have to take a detour. Lied to myself. Wanted her in my car.

"Okay, let's go!"

Hit the accelerator. Back tires burnt up the road. We were on our way.

"I'm Kate. Thanks again for picking me up. I don't usually hitchhike."

"That's okay," I responded. "So where are you from?"

"I'm not from around here, if that's what you're asking," she said with glee. She was extremely happy. How could she be happy in this heat?

"That's good. I'm just late to my meeting. I'm on my way to a convention, actually." That was right. Suddenly had a thought of being late to a convention.

"Fucking finally," she said.

We drove for some time without speaking. She kept looking at me. Yeah, I wasn't ugly, but this felt weird.

Awkwardly asked her, "So where are you going?"

"Oh, I'm going to a show. I got tickets to it and I totally forgot, and my car broke down." Funny—didn't remember seeing her car, I thought. Then she continued, "I waited out on the side of that highway for someone to take me down, and luckily you were there. Hey, can we stop by and get something to eat? I'm starving."

Looked at the time. Damn watch was broke. Had 10:41:03 on it.

"What time do you have?" I anxiously asked her.

"I don't carry a watch."

"Okay," I replied.

As we drove down the highway, for some reason it kept going downhill. Saw a sign on the left:

DINER NEXT EXIT

"Hey, look. There's a diner next exit. We can go there."

"Sure," replied Kate, looking outside.

We surely reached the turn and turned into the exit. There was a sign:

WRONG WAY GO BACK

"Hey, did you see that sign?" I asked.

"No, I didn't."

The radio started playing static.

shhSHHHSHHHHHH

The sound was deafening.

"The radio doesn't work," I said.

"I didn't touch anything," she said.

Turned it off.

There was a small diner with a half-hanging sign —"Colin's Diner"—swinging on one hinge, metal creaking with each swing even though there was barely any wind. A tumbleweed rolled across the parking lot, the only thing moving in this dead place.

Parked the car and looked across at Kate. She was already halfway out of the car, on her way inside.

"Let's go, I'm starving," she said.

We entered the diner. Empty tables and one man at the bench. He looked old and had a hat with his head down. The place was clean. Too clean. The outside didn't match the interior. It looked like it had been newly built—bright red and white, just like the ones in the old movies.

Walked to the table with Kate. "Let's take this seat," I said.

A woman—old frame—walked out of the kitchen with her neck angled down. Thought she was looking down, but she walked that way, taking steps awkwardly forward. Could hear her groaning.

Looked at Kate and she looked at me with a look of disgust. Once she realized I saw her, her face changed to a neutral look.

Looked up and the old lady was next to us. How did she get here so fast? She just stood there without moving, looking down.

"Could I get a club sandwich? And what would you like?" I asked Kate.

She was staring at me again, then said, "Oh, I'll get that as well."

Kate then got up and started walking away.

"Where are you going?" I asked.

"I'm just going to the bathroom," she replied.

The old lady was walking away without even acknowledging us.

Looked around to see this place. Never been to a diner before, but I noticed something strange—the place had aged since I got there. It wasn't as bright as when I first walked in. The red was duller now, more rust than cherry. The white tiles had yellowed at the edges. The chrome had tarnish I swore wasn't there two minutes ago.

What the hell was going on? It suddenly got darker. But what was the time? Looked down and the watch showed 10:41:03. The damn watch was broke.

Outside began to get dark and cloudy. The wind picked up. Could hear the hissing.

Heard footsteps and the waitress was coming back with two plates. Looked in front where Kate was. Who takes this long in the bathroom?

The old waitress just stood there.

"Hello?" I asked. "Can we have the food?"

From the angle I was sitting, I could see flies flying around the plates. Slowly stood up and noticed that the plates had black tar-like sludge on them. Looked like there were maggots.

"What the fuck is that?" Stood back. Didn't know how to respond.

That's when I heard her laugh. It started slow, almost like a growl, then slowly grew to a laugh. She was shaking.

Slowly started walking backwards with my hands out. "I don't know what's wrong, but I'll be leaving now."

"Yooouurr nooot gooing annnywhere," an old, witch-like voice said. Her head then suddenly twisted towards me. Then I saw her eyes—they were white. Her smile from ear to ear. Literally fucking ear to god damn ear. Then she started getting taller. How the hell? Looked down and she was floating. Her head then started to crack and vibrated all in the wrong ways, and suddenly moved back—all the fucking way back—with her mouth open.

"You can stay. You can play with me. Let me suck your cock. You like that, don't you, you dirty motherfucker."

As she spoke, she turned towards me. She floated towards me.

Fell backwards. Screamed, "KATE! WHERE ARE YOU!?"

As I screamed, the monster of a lady started opening her arms and her fingers were long—as long as my forearm—and there were fingers on her fingers.

"What the fuck, what the fuck."

Fell and slipped on something. Touched it and it was goo. Looked up and the ceiling of the diner was covered in mouths. Long, elongated mouths, all with their tongues flicking.

"Cum inside me, cum. Let me bite your cock off. You don't need that anymore."

The voice was the same as the lady.

Then I heard it.

A thud.

Looked over at the bar stool. The old man—the one who'd been sitting there the whole time—fell. Just collapsed forward off the stool and hit the ground hard.

He didn't move like a person. Didn't try to catch himself.

Just fell.

And then he started gliding.

Toward me.

Not crawling. Not dragging himself with his arms.

Gliding. Sliding across the floor like something was pulling him.

His body flat against the ground, face down, arms at his sides.

But moving. Fast.

And behind him—a trail. Thick. Dark. Blood and goo smearing across the white tiles, streaking behind him as he slid closer.

The smell hit me. Rotten. Wet. Sweet and putrid.

He was getting closer. Ten feet. Five feet.

That's when I saw it.

The top of his head.

There was an opening.

Not a wound. Not a crack.

An opening.

Fleshy. Pink. Wet.

It looked like—

Oh god.

It looked like a vagina.

But wrong. All wrong.

The edges were lined with teeth. Small. Sharp. Rows of them circling the opening.

And it was opening and closing. Pulsing.

Like it was breathing.

it was hungry.

The man's body slid right up to me. Right between my legs.

The head tilted up. The opening faced me.

And it spoke.

The teeth gnashing with each word.

"Let me bite your cock off."

The voice was wet. Gargled. Like it was speaking through blood.

"You don't need that anymore."

The head lunged forward, snapping, teeth clacking together.

I kicked. Scrambled back. My hands slipping in the goo.

"KATE! WHERE ARE YOU!?"

The head kept snapping. Closer. Closer.

The trail of blood and goo spreading wider.

And then—

Nothing.

Looked down to see the old man and he was gone.

Looked up and the ceiling was back to normal—just ceiling, just tiles, no mouths. The old lady was gone.

The diner turned back into its shiny new self, bright red booths, gleaming chrome, like I'd imagined the whole thing. But my hands were still wet with that goo. Could still smell it—sweet and rotten, like fruit left in the sun too long.

Kate had come back, walking towards the table.

"Hey, why are you on the floor?"

"Didn't you—I mean, didn't you see, see that?" I fumbled. Looked around. What the fuck was going on? What happened just now?

Stood up and looked around. Then I saw the old lady slowly walking back with the food. She came towards the table.

"Stay the fuck away from me!" I screamed.

Kate laughed. "It's just a sandwich."

She then put the food on the table and waddled back into the kitchen.

Kate took a bite from the sandwich. "What's the matter? Sit down and eat."

"I'm not hungry," I said nervously, looking around. The guy was still sitting on the bar stool.

"I'm going outside. I'll wait for you in the car."

"Jason, are you okay?"

"Yeah, yeah, I'm fine. I'm going outside. I'll wait for you in the car."

"That's okay. I'll come with you. This tastes like ass anyway," she replied.

We got back in the car. Had to catch my breath for a moment.

"You okay?" asked Kate.

"Yeah, I'm okay. Let's go. I need to be at this meeting."

"Sure, Jason. Let's get out of here."

Put the car in reverse, then headed back to the highway. Looked in my rearview mirror and the old waitress was staring through the glass of the diner.

What the fuck was going on!?

"No more stopping, Kate. I am really late."

"Yeah, sure," she replied.

With that, I saw a flash of light near the red glowing light.

We traveled down the dusty highway. Kate looked at me and said, "What happened there? Why were you freaking out?"

"You wouldn't believe me even if I told you," I said.

"Anyway," she said, "let's listen to the radio. You got a favorite station?"

"No, I don't. I don't really listen to the radio. Let's try Hits Station 1.041. I heard it's really good."

CHAPTER 4
Suki

We drove down the highway, my mind still traumatized by the diner. There were no signs of getting closer to our destination. It always felt like it was going to take forever to get there. The road just kept stretching. Same dusty pavement. Same hot fog hanging over everything. Same red glow in the distance that never seemed to get any closer no matter how fast I drove.

Then, out of the blue, Kate asked me a question. "So Jason, are we going to talk about what happened back there? Why were you freaking out?"

I snapped at her and it made her jump. "I told you I don't want to talk about it, okay? Today's been absolutely strange from the moment I woke up until now. I don't know what's happening to me. I also don't remember yesterday. All I remember is lying in bed and waking up." I left out the parts where I shit my pants.

"Well," she replied, "that's interesting. Maybe none of this is real." Then followed it with a laugh.

"Honestly, I am starting to think I'm still dreaming."

"Well, my mum used to say if you pinch yourself you will wake up from a dream. Go on, try it."

"What do you mean? Like pinch myself?"

"Yeah, that's right," she said.

"Sure." I pushed my knees up to hold the steering wheel steady, gave my arm a pinch. "Nothing. This is definitely real."

"Let me try," she said.

And with that, she grabbed the skin on my arm and dug her nails deep into my arm. Her nails were sharp. Too sharp. They broke skin immediately. I could feel warm blood running down to my elbow.

I felt excruciating pain.

"What the fuck's wrong with you?!" As I grabbed my arm, the car swerved on the road. I quickly gained control.

"Oh, sorry. Didn't realize that hurt."

"Of course it fucking hurt. Seriously, you're crazy."

"Only a little," she said, then smiled and smirked.

"Hey, look at the smoke ahead."

"I'm not stopping for anyone, I'm serious," I told her with frustration.

But look—as we got closer, there was a car. An old car, similar to mine, that had the hood open with smoke and flames rising out aggressively.

There was a small Asian lady standing behind the car, waving her arms around.

"We should stop and help her," said Kate.

The moment I saw her, something happened. I felt strange. She was so sweet and cute and vulnerable. I needed to help her.

"Sure," I said. "We can see what's going on."

I approached the girl and as I pulled over next to her, she was short—like an anime character. She was a small cute Asian lady around 21 with bangs. She was in a white Lolita-style outfit. Too clean for someone who'd been outside waiting in this place. The white dress didn't have a single smudge of ash or oil on it. Her hair was perfect. Not a strand out of place despite standing in the heat and smoke.

"Hey," I said. "Are you okay?"

I spoke over Kate as she leaned back to let me talk with her.

"Hey," a cute voice replied. "Thanks so much for stopping. I don't know what happened." She said in a Japanese-English accent. "My car just went boom boom." Then she smiled with her crooked canine tooth.

"Boom?" I replied, replicating her hand motions.

"Haha, hai," she replied.

"Where are you going?"

"I go there," she said. "Same to you?" she asked.

"Yes, we go there." I pointed to the red glow. "Come together?"

I asked her and she replied with a small bow, then got into the back seat. As soon as she got into the car, she put her seatbelt on.

"Okay, let's go. More the merrier."

Everything went quiet for a moment as I drove off toward the glowing red light. Too quiet. The engine was still running but I could barely hear it.

That's when the smell hit me.

Sweet at first. Coconut from Kate. Something floral from Suki—jasmine maybe, or lilies.

But there was something else underneath. Faint. Sour.

Like garbage left out in the heat. Or roadkill a few days old.

I wrinkled my nose. Cracked the window. Hot air rushed in but the smell lingered. My lips as dry as sandpaper. My throat just hanging on, trying to find moisture in my mouth. I'm so thirsty. I need water.

Weird. Must be something outside. Dead animal on the road maybe.

I glanced at Kate. She didn't seem to notice. Suki was humming something in the back seat, completely unbothered.

The smell got a bit stronger but I was getting used to it. It wasn't that bad, really. Almost sweet if you didn't think about it too much.

I cracked the window wider anyway.

Didn't help.

Whatever. Probably just the heat doing something to the upholstery. This car was old as hell.

As we drove, a sign appeared. This seemed to be the first sign since the diner.

ROAD CONSTRUCTION AHEAD TAKE DETOUR

The road was blocked by a—wait, is that a chair? A wooden chair just sat there in the middle of the damn road. I need to go see. I turned to the girls.

"Stay in the car, guys," I told the girls.

"Ah, okay, okay," said Suki.

Kate just gave a nod.

I got out of the car. Stopped just a few feet away from the chair. There was something strange about it. Why would there be a sign and this chair? I walked towards it. Surely I could move this. It was made from wood with clamps on each armrest. That's strange, I thought. I went to lift it away from the middle of the road. I could go around it but the signs were blocking the way.

I looked at my watch and the damn thing was still broken. For fuck's sake, it said 10:41:04.

I went to touch the chair and the moment I did, something happened.

Suddenly, everything went black. Then it came back. Then white. Black. White. Black. White. Faster. Like someone was flicking a light switch. My head felt like it was splitting open. The heat was unbearable. Couldn't breathe. Couldn't see.

What was going on with my eyes?

I tried to turn around to go back to the car, but the flashes kept getting faster and faster. I fell to my knees. What was going on? This shit hurt.

The girls didn't get out of the car. They were just staring at me. Through the windshield I could see them. Kate in the passenger seat. Suki in the back. Both of them perfectly still. Not concerned. Not worried. Just... watching. Like they were waiting for something to happen.

I was in a room. Not in the hot sun. Not on the ground. Lying down. Something restraining me. I couldn't move my arms.

I looked around—it was some kind of hospital. I could barely see. Something was on my head. There was a doctor checking my pulse, flashing a light in my eyes. Cold. Everything in the room was cold—the air, the surface beneath me, the hands checking my pulse. Antiseptic smell. Beeping machines. Fluorescent lights too bright.

People staring at me.

"No good," he said. "Hit him again."

Then suddenly I came back. Back on the ground. Back in the heat in front of my car. I was on my hands and knees. What was that? I asked myself.

I stood up, looking at the girls in the car, and walked towards them.

I opened the door, went in. They both stared at me.

"You okay?" Kate asked.

"Yeah, I'm okay." I didn't tell either of them what just happened.

"Why did we stop?" she asked. "Is it because of the tree?"

"What tree?" I asked, surprised. I looked forward. The road was blocked by a massive oak tree lying on its side. Unnaturally placed. There were no other trees around. Just this one.

"Yes. Well, because of the tree," I said, not wanting to sound crazy. "Where's the chair?"

"What chair?" Kate asked. "Are you dreaming again? There's a damn tree the size of a house blocking the road. You said you would check it out."

I looked ahead again. The tree was gone.

"Why did we stop?" Suki asked, her fringe shaking in the wind.

"Because of the tree," I said. I looked forward. The tree was gone. The road was open again. Like it was never there.

But my knees were still scraped from falling. The pain was real. The chair was real. The tree was real. Wasn't it? Which one was there? Am I losing my mind?

I need to keep moving forward. I can't keep stopping. I must have hit my head somewhere. Yes, I'm having a concussion. That's why I'm seeing crazy shit.

So with that, we hit the road again. Suki in the back seat, smiling, looking outside of the window, and Kate next to me.

"So guys, where are you both really going?" I asked, trying to change the topic. I don't want them to think I lost my marbles.

They both just stopped what they were doing and stared at me in silence, like I flicked a switch on them. A blink. Something was wrong with Suki's face—gray skin, sunken eyes, her smile stretching too wide and showing bone where flesh should be. Another blink. She was back. Cute. Perfect. Smiling like nothing happened.

"What do you mean? I go to the show," she said.

"What show?" I asked.

"The big show over there." She pointed to the red glow.

"And you, Kate?"

"Yeah, like I said, I'm going to the concert."

They answered at the same time. Exactly the same time. Same cadence. Like they rehearsed it.

"So you both are going to the exact same place?"

They looked at each other. "Yeah, I think so." They grinned, then looked at me and smiled.

"Let's not waste time. Go, go, go!" Suki said excitedly.

And that's when everything turned to shit again.

BANG.

Sound came from the engine which was then followed by flames, then the tires exploded. The car swerved to the side against the gravel, we spun and then came to a stop.

The fuck is wrong with this damn car? I'm sick and tired of this shit.

"You guys okay?" I quickly checked if the girls were okay. Like they were my possession of some kind. I felt ownership over them for some weird reason.

Kate gave a thumbs up and Suki nodded nervously.

"Okay, get out girls, we're walking."

CHAPTER 5
Bonjo

Got the suitcase. Kate and Suki both got out of the car. It was an absolute wreck—smoke pouring from the hood, tires blown. Turned and looked at the road. Sweltering hot.

"Okay girls, we walk. Or hitchhike, whichever comes first."

Walked and walked for miles without saying a word to each other. So hot the jacket and shirt came off, draped over one shoulder. Kate and Suki were trailing behind, walking like they'd done this before. The heat not bothering them at all.

"Aren't you guys hot?" Surprised at their comfort.

"No, it's okay," Suki said.

Kate just shrugged. "Not hot for me either." She made ghost sounds—"OooOOooO"—then laughed. "The heat must be for you."

God, she was crazy.

We walked for miles without stopping. All that could be seen on either side of the hot, sandy, fogged road were mirages. The heat tricking us into believing there was water or a lake ahead.

Then, ahead in the distance, a small building appeared. No—not a building. A single-floor shop in the middle of nowhere. A black box-like shop, getting closer and closer.

"Look, girls. Do you see that?"

"See what?" Kate replied.

"The house. Or shop. I can't tell."

Turned to look back at them. The building was right in front of us now.

How the—a moment ago it was so far away. Now it was here.

WELCOME TO THE MUSEUM OF WONDERS

The sign at the shop front. Windows tinted black. The door centered, bright red. The frame around the door made of gold with small gargoyle heads on each corner. The eyes on those heads felt like they were watching. Tracking movement.

The sign on the door read: OPEN

"Girls, I think we need to go inside. Get some water. Maybe ask for help."

Walked in. The cold air hit like a breeze. The most comfortable feeling all day. From all the horrific things endured, this was well deserved. Like a reward for suffering.

Inside was a counter with pigeonholes in the back, all full of different keys. Looked like an old hotel.

A sign on the wall pointed down a corridor: **THIS WAY TO THE MUSEUM**

Turned to the girls. "Do you wanna come with me to check out the rest of this place?"

"No," said Kate.

Suki shook her head. "I stay here. I stay with Kate."

"Okay. I'll be back. Just wait here."

Walked ahead down the corridor. Dark walls. Flickering lights overhead. That buzzing sound that made my teeth hurt.

Doors lined both sides. Each one had a placard at eye level.

The first one: **ROOM 1**

Hand already on the handle.

The door opened.

Darkness. Then a screen flickered on.

Not a screen. Something else.

An animatronic in the center. An old man. Arms out wide. His lower half—an octopus. Tentacles coiled underneath. His head split down the middle. Two halves hanging open. Organs spilling out. Wet. Moving.

It moved. Smooth. Like strings controlled it.

Bent down. Picked up a box.

Inside—babies. Moving. Squirming. Tiny hands. Tiny mouths.

Picked one up. Brought it to his mouth.

Stepped forward. Hit glass.

Put the baby in his mouth. Chewed.

Heard crying. Human crying. Children.

Pressed my ear against the glass.

"Please help us. Don't eat us. Please."

Pulled back. The thing still chewing. Still grabbing more.

Turned to leave.

The face.

Right there. Against the glass. Right in front of mine.

Didn't hear it move.

Split head inches away. Halves hanging open. Organs out. Eyes rolled back. Mouth stretched wide. Flesh in its teeth. Blood dripping.

It smiled.

The two halves tilted. Independent. Like separate things on one body.

I fell back. Hit the wall.

It stayed pressed there. Watching. Smiling.

Then dragged its tongue across the glass. Thick smear. Black and red.

Got up. Ran. Door slammed behind me.

Stood in the hallway. Heart hammering.

What the fuck was that?

The next door. Just feet away.

ROOM 2

Didn't want to go in. Something pulled me forward anyway.

The door opened.

Bright this time. Fluorescent lights. Everything visible.

Two animatronics in the center. A man and a woman. Wooden. Carved. Detailed. They had all the parts. Everything.

Stepped forward.

The woman dropped to her knees. Started moving. Mimicking.

Just wood. Nothing actually happening. Just motion.

Then their skin changed.

Wood grain faded. Became flesh. Pink. Real.

Human now.

She stood. Bent over. He moved behind her. Fast. Too fast.

Didn't think a human could move that fast.

Their skin turned gray.

Her sides split open. No blood. Just opening. Frogs came out. Dead frogs. Dozens. Spilling onto the floor.

The man convulsed. Something pushed out from behind. A baby goat. Wet. Newborn. Bleating.

A voice screamed in my head:

"Oh come on let's fuck let's fuck let me inside you I wanna cut you cut fuck fuck cut"

Not my thought. Something else.

They grabbed the goat. Ripped it apart. Started eating.

I backed toward the door.

Glass. There's glass. I'm protected. This is fake. Just a museum.

Gave myself false confidence. Turned. Left.

The wet sounds of chewing followed me out.

Back in the hallway.

Not going into any more of these fucking rooms.

Started walking back.

A bell rang.

From behind the counter came a sound. Knocking.

Went over. Looked down. A trapdoor. Knocking. Muffled voice: "Hey, open up."

Went to open it. Heavy. Pulled. Didn't budge.

"Girls, help me with this door."

They didn't move. Just staring.

"I would leave that closed," said Kate.

"Why?"

"Who knows? It's like one of those sex dungeons. Maybe you'll catch someone in the act."

Suki laughed.

Pulled again. The door gave in. Fingers came out. Man hands. Black nails.

Voice clearer: "Thanks. Can you let me in?"

"Sure. Let me pull again."

Pulled. Opened. Weight removed.

His head came up. Young. Handsome. Thin. Walked up the stairs. White business shirt. Black pants. Shiny black shoes. Like mirrors.

"Thank you for letting me in," the young man said. "I have been stuck down there for ages."

"Oh, hi ladies." He bowed.

Suki and Kate bowed back. Suki's more Japanese. Kate just tilted her head.

"My dear ladies, you look so thirsty and tired. The road outside must be so perilous and uncomfortable."

Pulled out two bottles of ice-cold water from under the counter. Gave them to the girls.

"Oh, thank you," said Kate.

"Arigato gozaimasu," Suki said with another bow.

"Do you have another one for me?" Desperation clear. So thirsty.

"Of course." Went back. Pulled out a shot glass. One for me. One for himself. "Let's celebrate this new friendship. I am Bonjo, the owner of this humble museum. You are?"

Pointed toward the girls.

"I'm Suki," she said. Another bow.

"Kate," she said. Grabbed the bottles and drank one. Suki took a sip from the other.

"Jason, you're not from around here, are you?"

"No, I'm no—wait. How did you know my name?"

Waved it off. "Heard you guys talking while I was stuck under there."

"Here, Jason. Have a drink."

Took the shot glass. Gave him a cheers. Put it to my nose. Smelled strange. Almost sweet.

Took a sip. He chugged his. Followed suit.

Nothing at first. No taste. No after-effects. Didn't taste like alcohol. Didn't smell like water.

Put the cups away. His movements fluid. Like water.

"Thank you for the drinks. We are heading off to the concert ahead."

"Oh, you don't want to go there now, do you? It's so hot outside. Come, stay here for a little, and then you can leave."

Put his hands on my shoulder. Felt heavy. Not with weight. With presence.

"Sure. We can stay for a while. I'm in no rush to get out in that heat."

"Wonderful!" Bonjo said, arms out.

"First, you guys get all washed up. Especially you, Jason."

Standing there with shirt off. Dusty. Dirty. The girls didn't have a speck on them.

These girls are my kind of girls.

Bonjo led us through the back room into a hallway. "Follow me this way, please."

The hallway looked like it shouldn't be attached to this shop. But it was there. Like every weird fucking thing today.

"These are rooms you can rest in," Bonjo said. Walking past closed doors with names on some. Ted. John. Donald. William. Earle. Juan. The last one—Ed. Old door. Wood swelled around the edges.

"Why are there names on the doors?"

"Oh, don't mind them. They are the old tenants' rooms. Your rooms won't have names on them, so don't worry."

Paused. "Well, at least not their names."

Laughed. Then stopped. Stopped walking. Came to the end of the hall. Three rooms. No names. New doors. Keys already on the handles.

"Here we are. Girls, these are your rooms. You may enter and rest. I'll come and get you for dinner later."

The girls went in.

Fuck, fuck, fuck. They don't love you. They don't need you. They wanna fuck Bonjo. They're gonna suck him, fuck him. You loser. You fucking LOSER!

Shook my head.

"You okay?" asked Bonjo.

"Yes. Sorry. Just have a headache."

Put his hands on my shoulder. Felt that weight again.

Looked at him. His eyes so blue. Almost too blue. Like a cat looking at prey.

"Now, Jason," Bonjo said, "I have some guests coming that I must deal with. So if you would, please clean up, rest up, and then I'll come by later to get you and the girls. But a word of warning—please don't leave this room."

"Why not?"

Leaned in close. The smell hit. He smelled so good. *Take a bite. Take a bite.*

Shook the thought out.

"Because the guests I have over don't like outsiders. They might—" Paused. "Act out. Just stay here until I fetch you all, okay?"

Smiled.

"Okay."

Turned the key. Heard Bonjo walking away. "Rest up," he said as he disappeared around the corner.

Opened the door. Went in. Closed it behind me.

Bonjo

What the fuck.

The same room from this morning.

What was going on?

CHAPTER 6
The Dinner

What was going on?

The exact same room. Looked around—the bed, the sheets, the colors. Everything identical. Only main difference: no door with windows.

How were all the rooms in this place the same?

Sat down on the mattress—hard as a rock. While I looked around, wondered why the hell I was here. That's when I heard a noise, a muffled sound coming from outside.

Got up to open the door to check. Turned the door knob.

Locked.

Pulled and shoved. Nothing budged.

Remembered what Bonjo said: "Because the guests that I have over don't like outsiders."

Did he lock me in to protect me?

Fucking cunt asshole. He wants us dead. He wants your balls. He wants the girls. Yes, the girls. He wants the pussy. He wants them both!

What the fuck was that?

Shook my head again. The voice got louder.

Looked around the room. Pretty empty. A mini fridge —old, overused. The bed—sheets looking like they'd never been cleaned.

That's when something strange caught my eye.

On the table. A rolled-up cloth on the bench top. Looked like something hard inside.

Rolled it open.

Full of stainless steel surgical equipment.

A scalpel. Number 3. Number 4. The Kelly forceps CVD—hadn't seen that in a while. The Spencer scissors. And my all-time favorite: the curved 22cm bone cutter.

Oh wow. A bone saw. Angled. Six-inch. That was a classic.

Wait a minute.

How did I know these?

Dropped the bone saw back on the table. Sat back down, wondering how the exact names of all those tools were known.

Wait. This made sense.

Had a vision. A doctor performing surgery.

Wait. Was that me? Was I the doctor?

A doctor?

With that, stood up. Tried to close my eyes and imagine performing surgery.

Suddenly, a flood of new memories.

Hands covered in blood. Cutting into a woman's breasts. It was like a flash.

Another flash. A woman's face, sleeping. Cutting a throat. Must have been performing surgery.

It made so much sense.

Must be a doctor. An important doctor. Somehow ended up here.

It was all making sense now.

That's when the muffling noises of voices came from outside the door.

Sounded like Bonjo. "Right this way. Dinner will be served soon."

Walked up and peeked through the peephole.

Saw Bonjo walking past, holding a rope. He dragged a child along.

No. Not a child. A man with dwarfism.

He had a rope around his neck. Bonjo pulled him forward. Behind him, four people in black robes walked.

"This way. Dinner will be served very soon."

He disappeared around the corner. Heard the door close.

That wasn't strange at all. A midget being dragged with a rope. Must be some kind of sex shit. Who was I to judge? Each to their own, I guessed.

Let's get out of here. They want to stop us. They want to kill us. Get the girls and get out. They belong to me. To us. Let me in. I can get us out. I can free us.

No. Stop!

What was that damn voice? Who are you?

You don't remember us. We are you. You are us. We are the same, you and me. This place is trying to stop us, trying to control us. But us knowing better. We know better. We is a doctor. We is a fixer. We fix this thing now. We can.

Fix what? What are you talking about? You mean escaping?

We must leave this place and go back to the road and gets back to ours jobs. We busy we are. So many waiting. So many tired.

Shook my head. The stupid voice in my head got louder.

Everything went black. Lost balance and fell.

The next thing—eyes opened. Standing on the other side of the door. The door stood half open.

Wait. When did that happen?

Didn't remember opening it. Didn't remember walking out here.

Looked down. There was something in my hand. Small. Metal. Bent at an angle.

A tool? Where did this come from?

Dropped it. The metal clinked on the floor.

The hallway was darker than before. Or maybe it was always this dark and I hadn't noticed. The wallpaper looked worse—mold creeping up from the baseboards, spreading like veins. The air tasted wrong. Metallic. Like blood or copper. The walls felt like they were breathing. Expanding slightly with each inhale. Contracting. Alive.

Needed to find the girls.

Went to Kate's door. Pushed it open.

Empty.

The room was smaller than mine. Just a mattress on the floor. But it was pristine. No wrinkles. No indentation where a body would have been. Like no one ever slept there.

Tried Suki's room. Same thing. Empty. Pristine. Untouched.

They were gone.

Something rose in my chest. Hot. Sharp.

Anger.

Not the confused kind. Not the "where did they go, I hope they're okay" kind.

The other kind.

The kind that made my jaw clench. Fists tighten. The kind that said they left without permission. They were MINE. How dare they leave.

Wait. Why was I thinking like that?

But the anger felt... good. Focused. Like it was keeping me sharp. Keeping me in line.

Didn't question it. Just used it.

Find them.

Leave. Let's go. We must go out from this place. You see? Go now.

No. Not leaving them.

Started looking around. Walking down the hallway where Bonjo led earlier. Listened. Heard nothing.

Slowly opened the door.

Wait. The—the fuck. It was the same room. The one I came in with. The counter. The back rooms. The cellar.

Walked to the end. Passed the rooms. Opened the door again.

This time, a different room.

A dining room.

Brightly lit. Like a surgery room. The fluorescent lights buzzing overhead, too bright, making everything look washed out and clinical. The center had a metallic table with holes in the middle. Looked like a morgue table. Drainage holes for blood.

The smell hit. Antiseptic. But underneath—rot. Meat. Something dead and sweet.

Cold in here. Like a freezer. Breath visible in the air.

Heard sounds coming in. Had to look for a hiding place.

Looked. Found a wooden cupboard in the corner. Looked like it didn't belong in this room. But it was big enough to fit.

Quickly went inside and waited.

Not a moment later, I heard voices.

"So sorry for the delay, my guests. I apologize. I was kept away by something. But thankfully, I've been freed, and now we can feast. Please, sit. Take a seat. I will prepare the delicacies for you all."

Tried to see what happened out there, but couldn't see clearly. Used fingers to move the gaps between the wooden frames inside. Luckily, could make out four hooded people sitting with their faces facing down. Bonjo at the head of the table.

Heard moaning.

Looked toward the middle of the table, but the hooded person blocked the view.

A cracking sound followed. One of the hooded figures leaned over, struggling with something. The moaning got louder. Followed by a scream.

What the fuck was going on?

Bonjo took an axe and slammed it down. The next sound was a loud thud. Crunch.

Tilted head over.

Oh fuck.

That was the midget. Lying there with a fucking axe through his face. Still alive. Still moving. Blood pooling in the drainage holes. Gurgling. Choking on his own blood.

"Bon appétit," said Bonjo.

With that, each of the hooded people lifted their hoods and exposed their heads.

Burnt. Melted skin. Baby faces. That's right. Fucking baby faces on adult bodies. Smooth, cherubic features twisted and scarred. Eyes too large. Mouths too small.

Each one of the hooded figures grabbed an arm, stretching the dying man. One grabbed a foot. Another grabbed a hand.

With that, they made a gargling noise and proceeded to eat the poor bastard. While he was alive.

Crunching. Slurping. Wet tearing sounds.

Bonjo sat there watching, his face covered in blood splatter.

What the fuck was going on? Needed to get out of this place.

There was a digital clock on the wall. The time read 10:41:05.

Felt something at my feet.

A rat.

What the hell?

Tried to push it off, but it began to climb up my leg.

Bonjo looked toward my direction. Slowly stood up. Signalled to the others to continue eating.

One of the hooded men—baby, whatever they were— ripped off the midget's dick and began to eat the fucking thing. Blood spurting. The midget still twitching.

Oh fuck this. Out of here.

Jumped out of the closet. Ran past Bonjo, who looked in surprise.

The four baby-faced men stood up and shrieked. High-pitched. Inhuman.

Wasn't there long enough to hear what they wanted to say.

Ran out through the corridor. Back through the check-in counter.

Bonjo waited there.

But how did you—

Looked back to see what was going on. When I turned, his face filled my vision.

"Oh no. I told you not to leave your room, Jason. You have been naughty."

"Please. Let me go. I need to go. Where are the girls?"

"Oh, the girls? They said they had to leave. They are waiting for you at the end of the road, Jason."

Heard the shrieks getting louder. They came. Just around the corner.

"Please. Let me go."

"Listen to me," he said. "Whatever you do, don't look back."

The screeching became louder.

"Go. But don't look back. I'll be with you in a moment. Don't worry about the girls."

He put his hands on my shoulder. Came close to my ear.

"Run."

With that, saw the source of the shrieks. Four of them. Standing side by side. The small man's body parts hanging from their hands. One still chewed on an eyeball that exploded. White, bloody liquid went everywhere.

Bonjo put his hands aside. "Now, now. Let's not be angry. This is a friend of mine."

With that, the creatures started to attack Bonjo. Swiping at him.

Ran. Didn't look back. Went out the door into the sweltering heat. Ran. Ran ahead as fast as possible. Just ran until my lungs were burning and I had to stop.

Thought I ran for hours.

The road was hot. The sun was bright. The fog was everywhere.

That's when a car horn sounded from the distance. Coming from behind.

Stopped to look. A black car in the distance.

Wait. That was my car. Racing down with dirt and dust trailing behind. An arm waving.

Looked closer.

It was Bonjo.

How the fuck did he get here? What happened with those baby-head things?

As Bonjo slowed down, saw the massive smile on his face.

"JASON!"

He opened the door with a grin that went from ear to ear.

In the back seat, the two girls. Just waiting. Smiling back.

Bonjo jumped out and gave me a big hug. "I'm so glad you're okay."

"Wait. You came to help me? And you got the girls with you? Where did they go?"

Pointed to them.

"Don't worry about anything," he said, hands out wide, trying to embrace again. "I like you, Jason. Of course I'll help you."

He bowed. "I'm at your service."

"Then what the fuck was that before? You killed a midget. A fucking midget. I saw you crack his head open like a watermelon. Those things—" Getting anxious now. "They started eating him. Like, what the fuck."

He looked. Smile still there. Hand came onto my shoulder. His presence strong.

"Are you sure you saw what you saw? You really saw me killing a tiny man? Did you ACTUALLY see that?"

With that question, started questioning myself. *Maybe I—* An image came to mind. Him with four women sitting at a table. A big roast chicken in the middle. Them eating it together. Bonjo cutting it open. Smiling.

"Well, maybe I—"

Sat down on the ground with hands on my head. "What's going on? Where am I? What is this place? Why am I seeing all these things? Am I going crazy?"

With that, Bonjo knelt down and pulled me up.

"Look," he said. "Let's go to your destination. All will be explained there. Everything seems so confusing now, but I'll show you when we get there, okay? Everything will be okay. Let's go. But you have to drive because I can't take passengers where we are going. Only you can bring us." He pointed to the girls. "With you."

I accepted everything at that exact moment. I stopped asking questions. Just walked around the car. Went in. Closed the door. Saw the suitcase there. Started the car. Looked back. The girls smiled.

We left. Now four of us. Going to fuck knows where.

CHAPTER 7
Destination

We drove for what felt like hours. No one said a word.

Bonjo turned to me. "Jason, we are almost there. However, there are a few things you need to prepare before you arrive. And before you ask, yes, I will answer whatever I can. However, like I said, this is YOUR journey. The road ahead can only be taken by you."

"What do you mean?" I asked him. "The girls are coming, right?"

Turned to see them. They just looked back, silent. None of Kate's spicy personality—gone cold since getting back in the car. Suki didn't even bow or acknowledge me.

"You see," said Bonjo, "they aren't really here. You put them here."

"What do you mean they aren't here? They are right there."

As the words came out, I looked to the back seat.

They were gone.

Hit the brakes. The car stopped. Both hands gripping the steering wheel.

Turned around. The seats were empty.

No. No fucking way.

Reached back. Touched where Suki was sitting. The leather was cold. Like ice cold. Like no one had been there for hours.

"They got out," I said. "They must've gotten out."

The doors were still closed. Still locked.

My chest got tight. Couldn't breathe right. Heart going too fast.

"What do you mean? WHERE ARE THEY!?" The scream came out raw.

He took our girls. Our meat. They belong to us. Us. No, they belong to me. TO ME!

Bonjo looked over. "No, Jason. They don't belong to you."

He heard the thought.

"Yes," he said. "I heard it. And it's not your thought that's speaking. It's you, Jason."

Shut up. Tell him to shut up. We is ourselves. We aren't his control. He not control us.

My lips moved. Not my mind. It was me talking. Out loud.

"What's going on?" I asked him. "Please. Tell me. What am I doing here? Where am I supposed to go? And who are you?"

Blinked.

He turned into Kate.

Blinked again.

Suki.

Blinked again.

The farmer.

Again.

The waitress.

Back to Bonjo.

"It's me," he said. "It's all been me."

"But why? Why am I here? Why did you do this to me?"

He looked surprised. Stepped out of the car.

I did the same. Kept my eyes on him.

"ME?" He laughed. Almost cackled. "I did absolutely nothing to you, kind sir. All of this is your doing."

My voice went deeper. I frowned. "Why the fuck did you bring me here? Why you bring us here? Where are we going!?"

Shook my head. Something had taken over.

"It's okay, Jason. That's not another being. That's you. Let him out." He leaned closer. "Remember that drink I gave you? That's going to bring your true self out."

"My true self?"

"Yes. That's right. Because only he can cross over."

"Cross over?"

"Yes."

"It's time, Jason. It's time you know everything."

With that, he put his hand on my forehead.

Cold. Then hot. Then nothing.

The heat disappeared.

Gone.

The fog. The road. The car.

Destination

All of it.

Gone.

The ground underneath—gone.

No sensation of falling. Just nothing. Like floating but not floating. Like standing but not standing.

Tried to scream. Nothing came out. No air. No lungs. No sound.

The silence hurt. Not quiet. Wrong. Like something missing from the world.

Couldn't see anything. Not black. Not dark. Just nothing.

How long? Couldn't tell. A second? An hour? Time didn't work anymore.

Then something changed.

Weight came back. Ground under my feet.

Blinked.

Could see again.

A door in front of me.

Red door. Bright fucking red. Only thing with color.

Looked down. There was ground now. Black. Smooth. My feet on it. My body back.

But the air felt wrong. No temperature. Couldn't smell anything. Just empty.

Looked to the side.

Someone standing there.

Tall. Too tall. Thin. Too fucking thin. Like someone stretched him out.

Black suit. Cane in his hand.

His skin looked gray. Tight against his bones. Face like a skull. Eyes weren't eyes. Just sockets. Something glowing inside them.

His hands—just bones with skin. Long fingers wrapped around the cane. The cane looked old. Twisted wood. Silver handle shaped like a snake's head.

My stomach dropped.

What the fuck.

This thing wasn't human. Wasn't alive. Shouldn't exist.

But I knew who it was.

"Bonjo? Is that you?"

His skull face nodded. Slow. Like he had all the time in the world.

He pointed to the door.

The red door.

Started walking toward it. My legs felt weird. Like walking on nothing.

Looked back.

He hadn't moved. Still pointing. Long bony arm stretched out. The glow in his eye sockets pulsed.

Waiting.

Turned back to the door.

Reached out.

Touched the handle.

Cold. Metal.

It creaked open.

The other side was like something I had never seen before.

CHAPTER 8
Good Night

Walked through and was inside a theater—looked like a cinema. There was no stage, just a large white screen. Looked around, turned and saw Bonjo still pointing from the other side of the door. The door suddenly slammed shut.

Turned to see what he was pointing at. There was a spotlight on one of the front seats. Walked down the stairs to the chair and found my name—no, my full name—engraved in the wood of the old wooden seat. The carving looked ancient, worn, like it had been there for a hundred years.

"Jason Gutani, the surgeon"

Surgeon? Knew it. A doctor.

Sat in the chair. The spotlight went off immediately.

Could hear the rolling sound of film. Turned to see where the sound was coming from and saw two black-cloaked baby-faced creatures in the back preparing the projector. What the fuck. Sat low in my chair, hoping they wouldn't see me.

Looked to the front—on each side of the screen there was one of them. Both standing with their fucked-up elongated bodies, baby heads that just didn't belong. One looking in my direction, grinning with his teeth out. The other looking straight ahead.

The screen came on.

A video of a child playing on the grass in his nappy next to the sprinkler. An old man next to him looking at the camera. Wait, I knew that man—that was my pop.

Another video. A toddler walking with a woman and man holding him. That was my parents. I remembered them.

An older child, about seven or eight, sitting in front of a Christmas tree opening presents. Getting a He-Man toy. I remembered that toy.

The screen changed. Me again, but with freckles. Twelve years old. This was our BBQ. We had a pool and there was a girl next to me, a little younger. We were playing.

The screen changed again. A teenager, around eighteen. A friend's party. Walking upstairs with a girl.

Didn't remember this one—must be when I got my first kiss.

The girl smiled, took my hand, led me upstairs. A bedroom door opened. Jocks waiting inside. They grabbed me, laughing, holding me down. Pants pulled down. Naked from the waist down. Alcohol poured—burning, screaming. Something shoved. Pain. Tearing. They let go, pushed me toward the stairs.

Stumbled down. Everyone watching. Laughing. Pointing.

Ran off, looked back at the party, and disappeared.

What the fuck—didn't remember that.

The scene changed again. An adult going to his office, talking with a girl. Her face wasn't clear. She left and he was watching her. His face wasn't clear either, it was blurry. That wasn't me—didn't work in an office. A doctor.

After that she went to her car to meet with a man, kissed him. The man was watching in the rain, in the car park, just watching them. The girl went home with the man and the blurry man was outside again, watching them from the window.

Scene changed again. Why was I seeing this?

Right after the man left and the girl was going to bed, the dark blurry man went through the window. It was clearer now—he wasn't blurry anymore. Could see him from the back. The girl was coming out of the shower when he confronted her. She stood frozen. His arms out, trying to talk. What was in his hand? A knife—no, not a knife. A scalpel.

In one swipe he swiped at her and that's when the sound came on. Could hear the screams.

Why was I seeing this?

The girl—that wasn't just any girl. That was Kate. Oh no, KATE, what happened to you? Did this happen after you disappeared?

Looked up at the screen. For some strange reason I wanted to watch it. The scalpel cut into her arms— tendons, muscle, bone all out in the open. She screamed, kicked, and punched. He punched her multiple times until her eye socket collapsed and she passed out. He stood up, turned around, looked straight at the screen. No—at me.

Wait, that couldn't be... that was me. This was some kind of joke, right? I didn't do that!

That's when I was pushed down by some entity, held down, and my hands were strapped by something invisible. Tried to fight it but it took over my entire body—had no power to control myself. My head faced toward the screen. Tried closing my eyelids but they were being held open by something.

On screen, I continued to cut at Kate, slicing her, opening her up, taking out her organs. Left her there for dead, upside down, pinned against a wall with nails, her entrails all hanging out. Walked away.

My head turned to see Kate next to me—bloodied, dead, with her intestines in her hands. "You did this to me, didn't you?"

"No, no," I said. "I didn't. That wasn't me."

My head was forced to look back at the screen.

A young girl got off a plane, landed, holding a map. She was short, cute, smiling. That was Suki. She was walking to a taxi when a man stopped her and asked her something. She bowed and followed him. That man —that was me.

He turned, looked at the screen again. It was me. I took Suki in my car—a black Cadillac. She sat in the front seat in her Lolita outfit. Pulled the car over and she looked confused. This time she was looking at me with confusion. She tried to leave the car but the door wouldn't open.

That's when I grabbed her by the hair and dragged her out of the car across the driver's seat. She was kicking and screaming in Japanese, begging and crying. Started slapping her. Jumped on her and started choking her in the middle of the street. There was no one around—looked like a dirt road in front of a farmhouse.

Wait, I knew that farmhouse. That was the same one as before.

As she passed out, a farmer came out with a bat. Grabbed the bat and disarmed him. That was the same farmer as—memories of him killing that pig in front of me started to emerge.

Wanted to get off my seat but couldn't.

Took the bat and started smashing his face. He was knocked out from the first one but I didn't stop there. Kept hitting him until his head split into two parts—the top and the rest. His brains all over the dirt ground.

There were two dogs—large black dogs—barking. Grabbed the bat's grip again and hit the first dog. Died immediately. The other came and tried to attack but she was too slow. Swung that bat so hard it cut through the dog's fur and she fell and bled out.

Came back to the farmer and jumped on his chest. Broke through and crushed his ribs. His chest all open with the ribs coming out.

Started walking toward Suki, who was breathing but halfway gone. Jumped on her and strangled her. My face looked happy—eyes crazy, tongue out. Suki passed out but I didn't stop. Heard a CRACK and she stopped moving.

Went to the car to take out a black cloth. Rolled it out —surgical equipment. Took it out and started slicing Suki from her neck all the way down to her belly button.

My eyes were being held open but this time I could see it wasn't an invisible entity. There was one of those baby-head creatures holding my left eye open. Another opening my right eye. One knelt down holding down my right arm, another my left arm. Couldn't move— they were so powerful.

Looked back up. The screen showed Suki upside down with her insides out, hanging against the farm shed. The shed—I suddenly remembered the smell of blood. The farmer was left there with his dogs.

The scene changed again. It was black. Looked around to see what horrible things they were going to show me.

A white room. Wearing an orange jumpsuit. Hands and legs chained. Head shaven. They sat me on a chair—the name "Sparky" carved on it. They put a wet sponge on my head and blindfolded me.

Across from me was a curtain and a clock. The curtain opened. There were people crying, angry, screaming. One man stood to point and shout at me. Another woman sulking, crying. They proceeded to lock me up and I said something—it was mumbled, couldn't hear it clearly—but a smile appeared on my face.

They stood back. The warden nodded his head.

I contracted violently. Shaking. My knuckles turned white.

It stopped.

The doctor came, checked my pulse, shook his head.

It went again. This time the jolts were less violent.

Once it was over, the doctor came and checked. Nodded his head.

The sound came up: "Time of death, 10:41 PM and six seconds."

A digital clock appeared above: 10:41:06

The entities let go—all four at the same time. But I still couldn't move.

Then from the corner of my eye, saw one of them holding something. My suitcase. Its arms stretched out, the case balanced on its hands. It walked over and put it in front of me. Just stood there. Staring. Waiting.

I knew the password.

Always knew it.

1

0

A click. Unlocked one side.

4

1

Second click.

Opened it slow. Careful.

Inside—face skin.

Sliced off. No bones. No skulls. Just the skin.

Kate's. The eye holes empty. Mouth hole stretched.

Suki's. Her skin pale. That crooked tooth gone—just the hole where it was.

The farmer's. Weathered. Wrinkled.

All three just lying there. Draped like wet cloth.

Then they moved.

The mouth holes opened.

Kate's skin spoke. Voice wet. Gurgling.

"You did this to us. Now we do this to you."

Suki's next. Broken English. Crying.

"I just come here. Now no more family. No more nothing."

The farmer's laughed. That same fucking laugh coming from a flap of skin.

"Hahahaha. You done now, boy."

The faces started crawling together. Skin sliding over skin. Merging. Eye holes multiplying. Mouth holes screaming.

They formed a ball. Wet. Pulsing.

Then it flew out of the case.

Straight into the screen.

The entities disappeared.

The screen split into two. The world around me was vibrating. Looked—Suki was on my right, laughing with her intestines out. Kate on my left doing the same, laughing and pointing. The farmer and his dogs standing near the screen. Dogs barking. Farmer laughing and pointing.

The screen and theater opened up. The red glow from the distance—now here. A dirt wall. It cracked and lava spilled out.

Still unable to move.

The heat hit first. Not like fire. Not like burning.

Like being inside the sun.

The lava touched my feet and my skin blistered immediately. I felt it—the moisture under my skin boiling, expanding, bursting. The smell of my own flesh cooking filled my nose—sweet, rotten, like pork left too long on a grill.

I screamed.

The lava climbed. Ankles. Shins. Knees.

Each inch was a new level of agony. My muscles cooked inside the skin. I felt them contract, tighten, tear away from bone. The tendons snapped like guitar strings pulled too tight.

"PLEASE! PLEASE LET ME OUT! I WON'T DO IT AGAIN!"

The lava reached my waist. My genitals melted. I felt them dissolve, the nerve endings firing all at once before they died. But they didn't stay dead. They regenerated. And melted again.

Over and over.

My stomach opened. The lava poured inside. I felt it fill my intestines, boiling them from the inside out. My organs swelled, burst, reformed, burst again.

I couldn't breathe. My lungs filled with molten rock. I choked. Drowned in fire.

Everything went black.

Then I was whole again.

Back in the chair. Strapped down. The creatures holding me.

No. No, please, not again.

The lava didn't come this time.

The dogs did.

They ran across the theater floor, their eyes glowing red, saliva dripping from jaws that opened too wide, teeth that were too long, too sharp, like broken glass.

The first one leaped. Its jaws clamped down on my face. I felt my cheekbone crack under the pressure. The teeth sank in, puncturing through skin, muscle, grinding against bone.

It ripped.

My left eye came out with the chunk of my face. I felt the optic nerve stretch, then snap like a rubber band. The empty socket screamed with pain even though there was nothing left to hurt.

But I could still see through the other eye.

I watched the second dog tear into my stomach. Its snout buried deep, pulling out ropes of intestine, shaking its head side to side like a toy. I felt every meter of my insides being yanked out through the hole in my belly.

The farmer walked over. He was laughing. That same pig-slaughtering laugh.

He grabbed his other dog by the collar. "Get the balls, girl. Get 'em."

The dog's teeth closed around my genitals. I felt each individual tooth pierce. Then it yanked.

The scrotum tore away. The testicles came with it.

I screamed so hard my vocal cords snapped. But the scream didn't stop. It kept coming, silent and endless.

The farmer knelt down, reached into the cavity where my genitals used to be, and pulled. He grabbed something inside—a nerve, a vein, I didn't know—and he twisted it like wringing out a towel.

I felt my spine light up with pain so intense I couldn't process it. Every nerve in my body fired at once.

Then Suki appeared. Sweet little Suki in her white Lolita dress, now soaked in my blood.

She held a machete. Rust covered the blade.

She smiled. That crooked tooth. "You did this to me."

She raised the blade high.

And brought it down.

It didn't go through clean. The blade was dull. It wedged into my skull, cracking the bone but not splitting it. I felt the pressure, the fracture spreading like ice on a windshield.

She wiggled the blade. Pushed harder.

My skull split.

I felt my brain exposed to air. The cold. The wrongness of it.

Kate appeared with a rock. The size of a bowling ball. Jagged edges.

She lifted it over her head. Her face was gone—just the bloody skull with her blue eyes still staring from the sockets.

"You took everything from me."

She dropped it.

The rock landed on the machete, driving it down through my brain, splitting my head in half like a melon.

I felt it all. Every inch. The blade cutting through gray matter, severing connections, slicing memories apart.

I saw flashes—my childhood, my parents, the party, the office, Kate's face as I killed her.

Then nothing.

Then I was whole again.

Back in the chair.

How long has this been going on?

It felt like hours. Days. Years.

The lava came again. But this time it was hotter. It didn't just burn—it vaporized. My flesh turned to steam before I could even scream.

The dogs came again. But this time there were dozens. A pack. They swarmed me, each one taking a piece. I felt myself being distributed, torn into a hundred wet chunks, each one still connected to my consciousness.

I was everywhere and nowhere, feeling every piece of me being chewed, swallowed, digested.

The girls came again. But this time they didn't just kill me.

They dissected me.

Slowly.

Carefully.

Like I had done to them.

Suki held my intestines in her hands, pulling them out meter by meter, measuring them. "Thirty-two feet," she said. "Did you know that? I learned that when you took mine out."

Kate peeled my skin off in strips. "You wanted to see inside me," she said. "Now I get to see inside you."

The farmer removed my ribs one by one with a crowbar. Each one cracked as it came free. He set them aside in a neat pile.

I begged. I screamed. I cried.

"PLEASE! I'M SORRY! I'M SORRY!"

Kate leaned down close. Her ruined face next to mine.

"Sorry doesn't bring me back."

She reached into my open chest and squeezed my heart.

I felt it contract under her grip. The blood stopped flowing. My vision went dark.

But I didn't die.

I just felt my heart being crushed, over and over, while I stayed conscious.

Then I was whole again.

How long?

How long have I been here?

Time didn't exist anymore. Just the cycle.

Good Night

Burn. Tear. Cut. Crush. Die. Wake. Repeat.

Over and over and over.

I stopped begging.

I stopped screaming.

I just endured.

The lava. The dogs. The girls. The farmer. The pain.

Again.

And again.

And again.

Each time a little worse. A little longer. A little more precise.

My mind started to fracture. I couldn't remember my name. I couldn't remember what I'd done.

All I knew was pain.

And that I deserved it.

Every second of it.

I was a killer. A murderer.

This was my eternity.

Ripped apart.

Reformed.

Ripped apart.

Forever.

Everything went black.

The pain stopped. The dogs, the girls, the farmer—all gone. No more lava. No more endless pain.

Me lying down on a motel room bed, with my dick out, choking to death. Oh what lows I had reached in my life to get to this fucking point.

CHAPTER 9
The Surgeon

A TV turned on.

Static first. Then a news desk.

Channel 7 News - Your Trusted Source.

A woman sat there. Middle-aged. Red lipstick. Pearl necklace. Professional looking. The kind of face that made you trust what she said.

"Good evening. I'm Linda Hartley with Channel 7 News. This just in—serial killer Jason Gutani was executed by electric chair tonight at the state penitentiary. After a three-year manhunt and a trial that captivated the nation, the man known as 'The Surgeon' or 'The 10:41 Killer' has been put to death."

She paused. Looked right at the camera.

"Gutani was convicted of brutally murdering two women—Kate Bexwilder and Suki Kosisaki—as well as pig farmer Richard Wright, who was killed while attempting to intervene. But investigators believe his reign of terror may have claimed more than fifty victims across the country."

The screen cut to crime scene footage. Police tape. Flashing lights. A farmhouse in the distance.

Linda's voice kept going over the footage.

"But what made Jason Gutani so dangerous wasn't just his brutality—it was how normal he seemed. Coworkers, neighbors, even police officers who interviewed him early in the investigation described him as quiet, polite, and helpful. The kind of man you'd never suspect."

CUT TO: Detective Morrison - Lead Investigator

A weathered man. Fifties. Badge clipped to his belt. Sitting in an interview room.

"Jason Gutani? When we first brought him in for questioning, I thought we had the wrong guy. He was cooperative. Polite. Answered every question. Even offered to help us with the case. He had this way of making you feel like he was on your side. Like he wanted to catch the killer just as much as we did."

Detective Morrison shook his head.

"Looking back now, that was the game. He was playing us. The whole time."

CUT TO: Susan Alvarez - Former Coworker

A woman. Forties. Glasses. Looked shaken.

"Jason was one of the nicest guys in the office. Quiet, yeah, but always helpful. If you needed something copied or filed, he'd do it. No complaints. Kate—"

Her voice broke.

"Kate was always nice to him. A lot of people ignored Jason or treated him like he was invisible. But Kate? She'd say good morning. Ask him how his weekend was. She was kind to everyone."

Susan wiped her eyes.

"And he killed her for it. Or maybe that's why he killed her. I don't know. I'll never understand."

BACK TO LINDA HARTLEY:

"According to court documents, Kate Bexwilder left work at 5 PM on the evening of October 12th. She went to dinner with her boyfriend, Michael Torres, who dropped her home at approximately 10:40 PM. What happened next would become one of the most horrific crime scenes investigators had ever witnessed."

The screen showed a photograph of Kate. Smiling. Blonde hair. Blue eyes. Alive.

"Jason Gutani cut the phone lines, entered through the back door—which had been left unlocked—and waited. When Kate emerged from the shower, he ambushed her with a surgical scalpel."

CUT TO: Sergeant Bill Kowalski - First Responder

A man in uniform. Jaw tight. Eyes looked far away.

"I've been on the force for twenty-three years. I've seen car accidents, domestic violence, gang shootings. But what I saw in that house..."

He stopped.

"It wasn't just murder. It was methodical. Surgical. He took his time. And when he was done, he displayed her. Upside down against the wall. Like she was a specimen. That's when we knew we weren't dealing with a crime of passion. This was something else."

BACK TO LINDA HARTLEY:

"But Gutani's killing didn't stop there. Just three days later, on October 15th, twenty-two-year-old Suki Kosisaki arrived at the airport to begin her new life as an international student studying fashion design. She never made it to campus."

A photo of Suki appeared. Smiling. Lolita dress. Holding a suitcase.

"Witnesses reported seeing a man approach Suki outside the terminal, claiming to be her pre-arranged driver. She didn't hesitate. She trusted him. She followed him to his car—a black 1960 Cadillac—and was never seen alive again."

CUT TO: Detective Morrison

"Suki's body was found seventy-two hours later during a welfare check on Richard Wright, a pig farmer living about thirty miles from the airport. When officers arrived at the property, they found Wright's body in the front yard. His skull had been caved in with a baseball bat. His two dogs—both dead. And in the shed..."

He stopped. Swallowed hard.

"Suki Kosisaki. Displayed the same way as Kate Bexwilder. Upside down. Organs removed. It was his signature."

BACK TO LINDA HARTLEY:

"Jason Gutani's capture came not from detective work, but from the instincts of one woman—Mariana Reyes, a hospital custodian who had cleaned the administrative offices where Gutani worked as a low-level clerk."

CUT TO: Mariana Reyes - Hospital Custodian

An older woman. Tired eyes. Rosary beads in her hand.

"I saw him in the hospital. Late. After hours. He said he was there to pick up paperwork, but I knew. I could feel it. Something was wrong with him. The way he looked at me. The way he smiled. It wasn't human."

She touched her cross.

"I told security. I told the doctors. They found him in the supply room, stealing surgical equipment. Scalpels. Bone saws. The same tools he used on those poor girls."

BACK TO LINDA HARTLEY:

"Gutani was arrested that night and charged with three counts of first-degree murder. But investigators believe his crimes extend far beyond what he was convicted for. Over fifty unsolved murders across twelve states share the same signature—victims displayed upside down with organs removed. And in every case, the estimated time of death was either 10:41 AM or 10:41 PM."

The screen showed a map of the United States. Red pins scattered across multiple states.

"Jason Gutani earned two nicknames during his trial —'The Surgeon,' for his precise and methodical killings, and 'The 10:41 Killer,' for his obsession with that specific time."

CUT TO: Dr. Elizabeth Crane - Criminal Psychologist

A woman. Fifties. Calm. Clinical.

"Jason Gutani fit the profile of what we call an 'organized serial killer.' He was intelligent, methodical, and able to maintain a facade of normalcy. People trusted him. That made him dangerous. He understood how to blend in. How to seem harmless. Unremarkable."

She paused.

"The fixation on 10:41 is troubling. It suggests a ritualistic element. A compulsion. We may never know what that time meant to him, but it clearly held deep psychological significance."

BACK TO LINDA HARTLEY:

"Tonight, at the state penitentiary, Jason Gutani was strapped into the electric chair—nicknamed 'Sparky' by prison staff—and executed in front of witnesses that included family members of his victims."

The screen showed the prison exterior. Dark. Ominous.

"His last words were inaudible. Witnesses report he was smiling."

Linda shuffled her papers. Looked down at her notes.

"The official time of death was recorded at..."

She stopped.

Looked down at her notes. Blinked. Read it again.

Her expression changed. Just slightly. Something flickered across her face.

She looked up at the camera. Hesitated.

"10:41 PM. And six seconds."

The studio went quiet.

She glanced down at her notes again. Like the numbers might change if she looked away and back.

They didn't.

Her voice got quieter. "The same time he killed his victims."

A pause. Too long for TV.

"10:41."

She stared at the camera. Not reading anymore. Just staring.

"Whether that was coincidence, or fate, or something else..."

Another pause.

"We may never know."

The screen faded to black.

But for a moment—one frame, maybe two—her face stayed visible in the darkness.

Still staring.

Still silent.

Then nothing.

A hand appeared. Skeletal. Long fingers wrapped around a remote.

Click.

The TV shut off.

The room went dark. No windows. Just shadows. The faint smell of sulfur.

A figure sat in a leather chair. Tall. Too thin.

Bonjo.

His skull face tilted. The empty sockets where his eyes should be glowed faint red.

He set the remote down on the armrest.

And smiled.

That same grin. Ear to ear. Split his face too wide. Showed too many teeth.

He leaned back in the chair. Stretched his long bony arms above his head.

Behind him, a wall of TV screens flickered on.

Hundreds of them. Thousands. Endless screens stretching into darkness.

Each one showing a different person. A different road. A different hell.

A woman choking in a bathtub. A man burning in a car. A child running through endless hallways.

All of them trapped. All of them looping. All of them his.

Bonjo's smile got wider.

He reached for another remote. Pressed a button.

One of the screens grew brighter. A new soul. A new journey.

He settled back into his chair.

And watched.

THE END.

AUTHOR'S NOTE

Since I was young, I've been haunted by 10:41.

Every time something significant happened in my life, it was 10:41 AM or 10:41 PM.

I lost my job at 10:41 AM. My neighbor died at 10:41 PM. My first real job interview was scheduled for 10:41 AM. The sports lodge I'm part of? Lodge number 1041. My favorite radio station? 104.1.

This number terrified me for thirty years.

When I started writing this book, I finished Chapter 1 at 10:41 PM. The next morning, I sat down to write again. It was 10:41 AM.

I wrote this book in six days because I needed to get it out of me. I needed to stop seeing it everywhere. I needed to make sense of it.

This number scares me.

I hope it scares you.

— David Gulasi

www.ingramcontent.com/pod-product-compliance
Lightning Source LLC
Chambersburg PA
CBHW040230170726
48295CB00014B/869